HOW ARE YOU FEELING TODAY BABY BEAR?

for children

Ladybird's Remarkable Relaxation
How children (and frogs, dogs, flamingos and dragons) can use yoga relaxation
to help deal with stress, grief, bullying and lack of confidence
Michael Chissick
Illustrated by Sarah Peacock
ISBN 978 1 84819 146 4
eISBN 978 0 85701 112 1

The Panicosaurus
Managing Anxiety in Children Including Those with Asperger Syndrome
K.I. Al-Ghani
Illustrated by Haitham Al-Ghani
ISBN 978 1 84905 356 3
eISBN 978 0 85700 706 3

for adults

Talking To My Mum
A Picture Workbook for Workers, Mothers and Children Affected by Domestic Abuse
Cathy Humphreys, Ravi K. Thiara, Agnes Skamballis and Audrey Mullender
ISBN 978 1 84310 422 3
eISBN 978 1 84642 526 4

Talking About Domestic Abuse
A Photo Activity Workbook to Develop Communication Between Mothers and Young People
Cathy Humphreys, Ravi K. Thiara, Agnes Skamballis and Audrey Mullender
ISBN 978 1 84310 423 0
eISBN 978 1 84642 533 2

HOW ARE YOU FEELING TODAY

BABY BEAR?

Exploring Big Feelings After Living in a Stormy Home

Jane Evans

Illustrated by Laurence Jackson

Jessica Kingsley *Publishers*
London and Philadelphia

First published in 2014
by Jessica Kingsley Publishers
73 Collier Street
London N1 9BE, UK
and
400 Market Street, Suite 400
Philadelphia, PA 19106, USA

www.jkp.com

Library of Congress Cataloging in Publication Data
A CIP catalog record for this book is available from the Library of Congress

British Library Cataloguing in Publication Data
A CIP catalogue record for this book is available from the British Library

ISBN 978 1 84905 424 9
eISBN 978 0 85700 793 3

Printed and bound in China

This book is dedicated to
my son, Jos, and the children, parents and carers
I have been fortunate enough to know and to work with
as they have all taught me so much.

Dear Child,

This story about Baby Bear is for you and for all the children who have had difficult things happening at home with the grown-ups they live with.

Baby Bear has some big feelings about the fighting and shouting between the grown-up bears, and needs some help to get these feelings out.

I hope this story will help you to find names for the big feelings you might have too, so that, like Baby Bear, you can have more 'sunshiny', good feelings and less 'rainy, stormy' ones.

With love from,

Jane

Once upon a time there were two Big Bears and a Baby Bear.
They all lived together in a house in the woods.

Baby Bear loved to chase butterflies, to make mud pies and to go to Nursery. This filled Baby Bear's tummy full of sunshine.

How do you think Baby Bear is feeling today?

Excited   Worried

Happy   Tired

Something else?

One night Baby Bear was asleep with Teddy the teddy bear, when some big sounds woke Baby Bear up. It sounded like a storm was happening downstairs so Baby Bear kept very still and hoped that the storm would soon stop.

How do you think Baby Bear is feeling?

Curious   Scared

Tired   Worried

Something else?

In the morning when Baby Bear came downstairs everything looked wobbly and messy. One of the Big Bears looked sad and the other Big Bear said nothing and went out.

After this, on some nights there were no downstairs storms but on other nights there were, with crashes, bangs, whooshes and sounds like the howling wind.

Baby Bear found it hard to sleep.

Then one day one of the Big Bears left the house for good. Baby Bear stayed living there with the other Big Bear and there were no more downstairs storms at night.

Baby Bear did miss the Big Gone Away Bear but not the scary downstairs storms and sad faces.

The next day at Nursery another Bear took Baby Bear's drink. 'Mine!' shouted Baby Bear, snatching the drink back and hurting the other Bear.

They both began to cry, so one Nursery Bear took care of the hurt Bear and another took care of Baby Bear.

How do you think the Bears are feeling?

Sad   Worried

Excited   Frightened

Something else?

'Goodness Baby Bear, are you OK?' asked Nursery Bear.
'You seem to have some big feelings today. I wonder what they could be?'

With help from Nursery Bear they talked about how Baby Bear was full of grey, rainy feelings on the inside and how these were to do with the downstairs storms and sad faces that had been keeping Baby Bear awake at night.

Nursery Bear listened and said it was time to talk with some other Big Bears to work out how to help make things better for Baby Bear.

After that Baby Bear still had days with grey, rainy feelings inside. Sometimes the rain leaked out and ran down Baby Bear's fur, making it wet and soggy. On other days Baby Bear would feel the tummy sunshine come out.

When the Nursery Bears asked, 'How are you feeling today Baby Bear?' after thinking for a bit, Baby Bear would say, 'a bit rainy today' or 'the tummy sunshine is out!'

So now Baby Bear finds words for feelings and has more sunny, happy feelings and fewer rainy, sad ones.

How about you? How are you feeling today?

How are YOU feeling today?

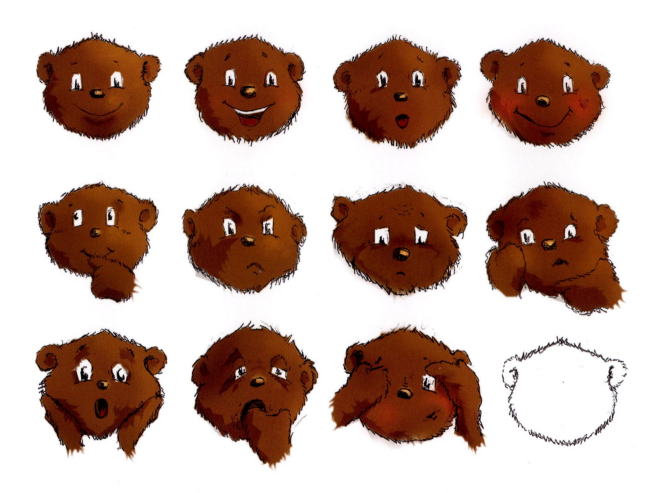

(Please feel free to photocopy this page to carry about with you for your child's pre-school, school or anyone else to use with them.)

Page by Page Guide to Using the Baby Bear Story

When children are repeatedly scared at home, especially in their early years, they form memories of the frightening sounds, smells, sights, and even touches. These memories stay in their brains and bodies and are known as 'implicit' memories, which are not able to be made sense of by a young child.

Using the book may help to give a child the words to describe the big feelings they have so that memories can become 'explicit' and outside of them, and more comfortable to live with as a result.

Page 1 It is helpful to let the child tell you about where they lived and who they lived with, as this may have been in a variety of homes, including a safe house, and with different people.

Page 2 Looking at what Baby Bear likes may act as a reminder of what the child had to leave behind: their pre-school or Nursery, toys, pets, people, the abusive or 'scary' parent. It's good to listen and not assume to know how they feel about this as they may have a mixture of feelings.

Page 3 Gently explore how Baby Bear may be feeling, by looking at Baby Bear's expression. Be guided by the child's suggestions and encourage them to think about what might have helped Baby Bear (e.g. the noises stopping, telling someone how they felt, being able to fall asleep).

Page 4 A child may, or may not, have seen chaos and upset the next day, as it could have been all cleared away and everyone may have acted as though everything was fine. This could have been confusing for them so they may respond to this page in a variety of ways.

Be careful not to assume that they felt upset with the Bear who is seen leaving, as the child may interpret the Bears in a different way. For example, the crying Bear at the table could be the 'scary' Bear saying how sorry they are, and the Bear leaving the house may be the other Bear going off to work.

Page 5 Discuss feelings around sleeping and bed times. Often the scariest sounding things will have happened at night when the child was alone in bed, left to imagine the worst, so they may be frightened and anxious and reluctant to sleep alone. What do they think might help now?

Page 6 Together, think about what can happen when a child has too many big feelings and worries. Don't focus on 'bad' behaviour, or what Baby Bear has done. Instead, look at what Baby Bear could do differently next time someone snatches things away and there are 'big feelings' for all concerned.

Page 7 Encourage the child to think about the feelings of both the Bears involved. This will help them develop the ability to care about and understand their emotions and the emotions of others. Often, a child growing up with difficult behaviour from the grown-ups in their home will not get this kind of input and opportunity and therefore may lack the ability to understand their own and others' feelings.

Page 8 It is important not to assume that Baby Bear feels relieved or glad when the 'scary' Bear leaves. Baby Bear may feel sad because they loved Big Gone Away Bear and had some positive times with them too, so they may experience a mixture of feelings.

Pages 9 and 10 It's time to discuss the range of feelings we all have and how they can change throughout the day. We rarely feel just one feeling at a time and we all need ways of moving on from uncomfortable feelings by learning to recognise and name them.

Photocopy **Page 10** as a feelings guide for when words can't be found, or to discuss something which has happened. Keep several copies around so it's easy to find and use throughout the day, either at home or at pre-school/school.

Activities and Games to Encourage Children to Explore and Learn About Feelings

Feelings Jenga

A parent I was lucky enough to work with gave me this idea, so a big 'thank you' to her.

Materials: inexpensive Jenga-type game, sticky labels, small figures, paper, pens

Use an inexpensive Jenga game, which can be found in a range of shops. On some of the bricks draw a face with a feeling on it and/or write the word for it too.

When someone pulls out a block with an emotion on it, they can talk about what the feeling means to them and/or what it looks like. If they enjoy acting things out, encourage this, or have some small figures or animals to use instead; or they may prefer to draw a picture about the feeling.

Most children I know love Jenga because it is a fun and easy game. Don't worry if they seem to lose interest quickly – this game can be quite hard as the children have to think about feelings which they may find upsetting or difficult.

Alternatively, you could put stickers with emotion faces on to plastic building bricks and build something using them, talking as you build, or you could stick faces on the back of an inexpensive puzzle and talk about them as you make it together.

Paper Plate Masks

Materials: pack of paper plates (not too thick), pre-cut eye holes, felt pens, lolly sticks, sticky labels/tape, glue/glue sticks, craft materials, elastic to go around head

Ask the children to decide which feeling they would like to make a mask about – angry or happy are popular! Encourage a discussion about what the feeling could look like and where we might feel it in our body. With the mask on they may want to role-play the feeling with you, or to you as their audience.

Playdough Pounding

Materials: home-made or shop-bought playdough

Most children love playdough and it can be great for calming a child down when you feel they may be having a difficult time. After pre-school/school, or following on from a difficult visit or session with someone, the repetition can be soothing and help them to relax.

I use the tune of 'Here We Go Round the Mulberry Bush', as it's one I easily remember, but you can use whichever tune suits you both best!

Whilst carrying out the actions, sing:

> This is the way we pat the playdough
> Pat the playdough
> Pat the playdough
> This is the way we pat the playdough
> On a cold and frosty morning
>
> This is the way we squeeze the playdough
> Squeeze the playdough
> Squeeze the playdough
> This is the way we squeeze the playdough
> On a wet and windy morning

This is the way we roll the playdough
Roll the playdough
Roll the playdough
This is the way we roll the playdough
On a bright and sunny morning

This is the way we stretch the playdough
Stretch the playdough
Stretch the playdough
This is the way we stretch the playdough
On a cold and frosty morning

This is the way we pound the playdough
Pound the playdough
Pound the playdough
This is the way we pound the playdough
On a wet and windy morning

This is the way we pat the playdough
Pat the playdough
Pat the playdough
This is the way we pat the playdough
On a bright and sunny morning

You can change the words and actions to mirror the child's needs and reactions, but try to end on a soothing note if possible.

Don't worry if they don't initially join in as they may need to watch you and just like listening to the singing, which will have a soothing effect on its own.

Emotions Strips

Materials: card, pens, elastic band/hair elastic

On each child-cut strip of card, draw a simple face for emotions they commonly know and a few you are teaching them. Write the words for them as well.

These can then go everywhere with them and with you. They can keep them in their school bag, pocket or by their bed so they can find the feelings they have and show you or leave it somewhere for you to see in the morning.

You can use yours to show how you are feeling too as visual cues are important for all children.

Note: Any work about feelings can be tiring and overwhelming for children who may not feel comfortable or familiar with it so go at their pace even if they can only manage a tiny amount to start with. If possible do some physical activity with them afterwards to burn off any stress, and give plenty of hugs too!